For Julia and Abigail
—D. C.

For Doreen
—S. M.

visit us at www.abdopublishing.com
Reinforced library bound edition published in 2009 by
Spotlight, a division of ABDO Publishing Group, 8000
West 78th Street, Edina, Minnesota 55439. This edition reprinted with permission of Atheneum Books
for Young Readers, an Imprint of Simon & Schuster
Children's Publishing Division, 1230 Avenue of the
Americas, New York, New York 10020. Text copyright
© 2007 by Doreen Cronin. Illustrations copyright ©
2007 by Scott Menchin. All rights reserved, including
the right of reproduction in whole or in part in any
form. Book design by Ann Bobco. The text for this book
is set in Bliss. The illustrations for this book are ren-
dered in pen and ink with digital color.
Library of Congress Cataloging-in-Publication Data
This title was previously cataloged with the following
information:
Cronin, Doreen.
Bounce / Doreen Cronin ; illustrated by Scott Menchin.
p. cm.
Summary: Rhyming text offers advice on the best ways
for toddlers to bounce.
[1. Jumping—Fiction. 2. Toddlers—Fiction. 3. Stories in
rhyme.] I. Menchin, Scott, ill. II. Title.
PZ8.3.C879 Bou 2007
[E]—dc22   2005037128
ISBN 978-1-5996-14229 (reinforced library bound edition)

All Spotlight books have reinforced library bindings and
are manufactured in the United States of America.

BOUNCe
doreen cronin
scott menchin

atheneum books for young readers   new york · london · toronto · sydney

C'mon!
Let's **bounce**
like a bunny!

hip

hop

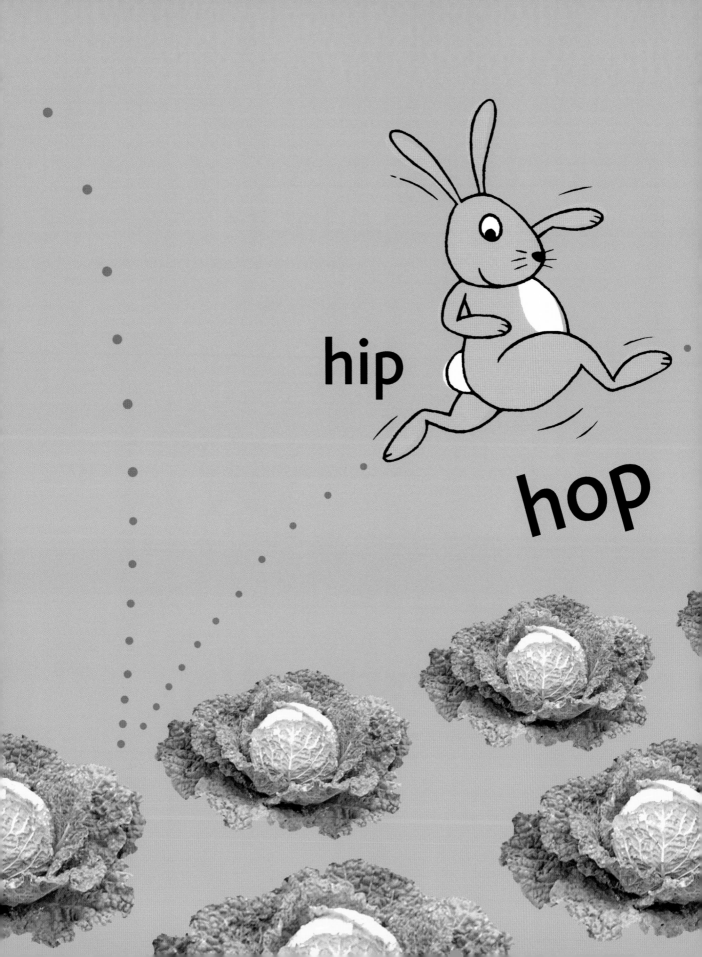

hip

hop

Let's
bounce
like
a frog!

ker- plop

I'll bounce to the left . . .

if you'll bounce to the **right**.

Bees
bounce
in
the
daytime.

Bats bounce in the night.

or bounce it off your toes.

I can
bounce a
beach ball
on the tip
of my
nose!

If you
bounce
into a
puddle,

it's best to bounce in boots.

If you
must
bounce
in
the
market,

Bouncing with your **best friend** is called a **bouncing** double.

Bouncing on the couch
is called **big** bouncing
trouble.

It's **hard** to bounce in roller skates,

it's **fun** to bounce on poles.

imagine all the holes!

bounce
back
into
the
shade.

If
bouncing
makes you
thirsty,

bounce

yourself

to **lemonade.**

A bounce can turn into a **bump**,

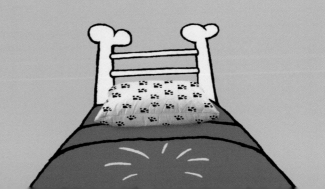

But it's better to have **bounced** and **bumped** . . . .

than **never** to have   **bounced** at all!